MATERIALS

ADVENTURES IN
STEAM

Claudia Martin

WAYLAND
www.waylandbooks.co.uk

First published in Great Britain in 2017 by Wayland

Produced for Wayland by
White-Thomson Publishing Ltd
www.wtpub.co.uk

Series editor: Izzi Howell
Designer: Rocket Design (East Anglia) Ltd
Illustrations: Rocket Design (East Anglia) Ltd
In-house editor: Julia Bird

ISBN: 978 1 5263 0474 2
10 9 8 7 6 5 4 3 2 1

Wayland
An imprint of
Hachette Children's Group
Part of Hodder & Stoughton
Carmelite House
50 Victoria Embankment
London EC4Y 0DZ

An Hachette UK Company
www.hachette.co.uk
www.hachettechildrens.co.uk

Printed in China

Picture acknowledgements:
Alamy: Paul Fearn 42t; AlexanderAIUS: 43b; Chemical Heritage Foundation: Harry Kalish 42b; Shutterstock: Max Halanskii cover and 1, R Nagy 3 and 40, Aleksander Krsmanovic 5, Art of Sun 6, Double Brain 7t, Robert S/NASA 7b, Versus Studio 8, Maria Uspenskaya 9, White Jack 10, Showcake 11, Yury Stroykin 12t, BCFC 12b, YanLev 13, R Classen 14, Beboy 15, Vagengeim 16t, Wallenrock 16b, Zeynur Babayev 17t, Bisams 17b, Johann Helgason 18, Natali Li 19, Grynoid 20, Marbury 21, Alexander Mazurkevich 22t, Krunja 22b, Syda Productions 23t, Photographyfirm 23c, Couperfield 23b, Bjoern Wylezich 24, Siaath 25, Andrey N Bannov 26, Pavel Ganchev 27, Li Chaoshu 29, Paul McKinnon 30, Vladimir Caplinskij 31, Mark Agnor 32, Whity2J 33, Structuresxx 34t, Wavebreakmedia 34b, Segen 35t, Baronb 35c, Cagi 35b, Fred Ho 36, Ostill 37, Pumidol 38t, Kamira 38b, FeyginFoto 39, 3Dsculptor 41, Svetlana Lukienko 43t, Ed Phillips 43c, Dalibor Danilovic 44, Evan Down Load 45.

All design elements from Shutterstock.

CONTENTS

CHOOSING MATERIALS

EVERYTHING AROUND YOU IS MADE FROM MATERIALS, FROM YOUR CHAIR TO YOUR CLOTHES. WHEN PEOPLE MAKE THINGS, THEY CHOOSE THE MATERIALS CAREFULLY.

Materials have different properties. Properties can be seen, measured or felt. When people choose materials, they look for particular properties. Here are some basic properties of materials:

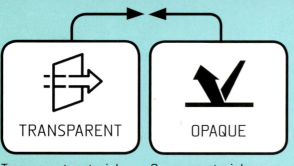

TRANSPARENT

Transparent materials, such as glass, water and air, are see-through, because light can travel through them.

OPAQUE

Opaque materials, such as wood, metals and rocks, cannot be seen through and they cast a shadow.

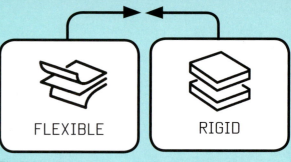

FLEXIBLE

Flexible materials, including clay, cloth and rubber, can be bent out of shape.

RIGID

Rigid materials, such as pottery, steel and seashell, cannot be bent. Unless they are strong, they crack easily.

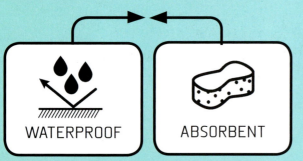

WATERPROOF

Waterproof materials include plastics, metals and glass. Water cannot pass through them.

ABSORBENT

Absorbent materials, such as paper, sponge and cotton, soak up liquids, including water, easily.

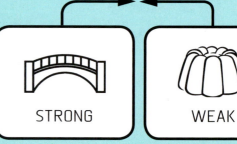

STRONG

Strong materials, including minerals such as diamond, and metals such as chromium, are hard to break or scratch.

WEAK

Weak materials, such as tissue paper, jelly and chalk, are easy to break or pull apart.

THINKING OUTSIDE THE BOX!

Think about the properties of the materials around you. For example, the glass in windows is transparent, waterproof and strong. Consider what would happen if the glass was swapped for an opaque, absorbent and weak material, such as sponge.

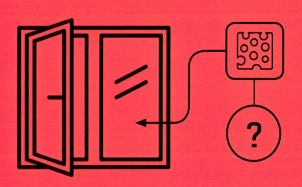

When we choose materials, we decide between natural and manmade materials. Our choice may depend on which materials are available locally and how expensive it will be to grow, mine or make a material.

— **NATURAL MATERIALS** are found in nature. Some are organic, which means they must be harvested from living things, such as animals and plants. Organic materials include wool and wood. Inorganic materials come from non-living sources and include rocks and minerals, such as gold and salt.

— **MANMADE MATERIALS**, including glass and plastics, are made in a factory or workshop. Their raw materials come from natural sources. For example, steel is a manmade metal made from a mix of iron and carbon, which are inorganic natural materials.

PROJECT

Divide the following materials into natural and manmade. Are the natural materials from organic or inorganic sources? With an adult's help, use the Internet to do some research.

BRONZE CALCIUM COAL

LEATHER PLATINUM

POLYESTER POLYSTYRENE

PYREX RAFFIA

RUBBER SILK

Many inorganic materials must be dug from the ground. This is a quarry where the rock granite is mined.

MATTER

ANOTHER WORD FOR MATERIALS IS MATTER. MATTER IS ANYTHING THAT TAKES UP SPACE AND HAS MASS. MASS IS A MEASURE OF HOW MUCH MATTER IS IN AN OBJECT. WE MEASURE MASS IN KILOGRAMS AND GRAMS.

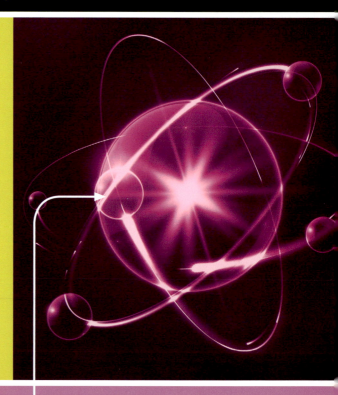

An atom has a nucleus surrounded by spinning electrons.

All matter is made up of tiny particles called atoms. The average atom is about 0.1 nanometres (or a ten-billionth of a metre) across. So far, 118 different types of atom have been identified. Materials made entirely of just one of those types of atom are called elements. The 118 elements are the pure, basic materials that are the building blocks for all other materials. Scientists list the elements in the periodic table, with the lightest, hydrogen, at number 1, and the heaviest, oganesson, at number 118.

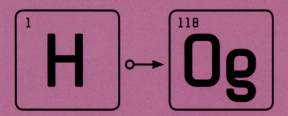

In the periodic table, each element's name is shortened: hydrogen is H, oganesson is Og.

SCIENCE TALK

Matter exists in different forms: solid, liquid or gas. These are called the states of matter. All the elements can be a solid, liquid or gas, depending on temperature. At room temperature, some elements are solids, some liquids and some gases. For example, silver is a solid, mercury is a liquid, and hydrogen is a gas.

There are only 118 elements, but the atoms in one element can join together, or bond, with the atoms in other elements. The new material is called a compound. This is how thousands of other natural materials are made, from water to salt.

Water contains two elements: hydrogen and oxygen. In each molecule of water, one atom of oxygen is bonded to two hydrogen atoms. A molecule is a group of bonded atoms.

OXYGEN

HYDROGEN

HYDROGEN

MATHS TALK

The most common elements in the universe are hydrogen and helium, which make up 98 per cent of all matter. All the other elements form the remaining 2 per cent. However, the make-up of the Earth is different from the universe as a whole: the element oxygen makes up nearly half of Earth's crust. Earth's rarest element is astatine. Less than 1 gram of astatine is found in the crust at any time.

SOLIDS

IF YOU LOOK AROUND, YOU CAN PROBABLY SEE MANY SOLIDS: FROM DESKS, PENCILS, PAPER AND CLOTHING, TO HUMAN HAIR AND FLOATING SPECKS OF DUST.

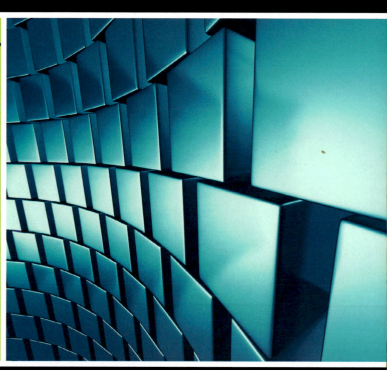

In a solid, the atoms are close together and joined in a rigid pattern. The atoms barely move: they just vibrate a little. They cannot be easily pushed aside, which is why you cannot put your hand through a desk. All solids share some basic properties:

SOLIDS

- can be held.
- have a definite volume, which means they always take up the same amount of space.
- have definite shapes. However, a few solids, like rubber balls, can be stretched or bent, and some, such as gold, can be hammered until they are flat.

SCIENCE TALK

Some solids float in water or other liquids. This property is called buoyancy. A material floats if it is less dense than the liquid it is placed in. Density is a measure of how tightly packed the molecules in a material are. The materials cork, wood and sponge float on water because they are less dense than water, while a metal ball sinks. So why do metal boats float? A boat is hollow: it is a wide bowl shape, filled with air. With its larger volume, a metal boat is less dense overall than an equal volume of water, and so it floats.

Another useful property of solids is the way they allow, or do not allow, energy to travel through them. Heat and electrical energy can only travel through solids by passing from atom to atom. This is called conduction.

○ Metal solids are good conductors of heat and electricity. The energy is passed quickly from atom to atom by tiny particles called electrons, which in a metal can leave their atoms and move about.

○ Other solid materials are poor conductors of heat and electricity, because they do not have free-moving electrons. Some solid materials, like plastics, are such bad conductors that they are used to stop heat and electricity from spreading. They are called insulators.

A metal pan is a good conductor of heat. The heat travels quickly from the pan's underside to the food. Metal pans often have plastic handles to stop heat travelling to the cook's hand.

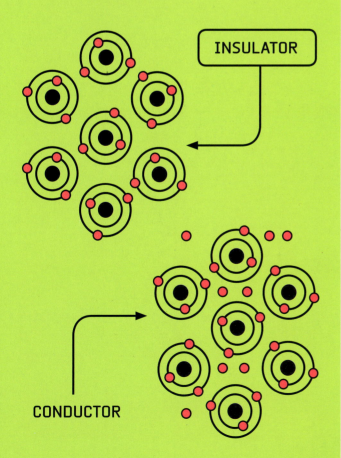

INSULATOR

CONDUCTOR

TECHNOLOGY TALK

The metal copper is an extremely good conductor of electricity. It is used for the wires that carry electricity through the walls of your home, supplying the energy for light bulbs and machines. The wires are coated with plastic for insulation. Copper wires also play a part in the Internet. They often carry the electrical signals that pass information from computer to computer.

LIQUIDS

AT HOME, YOU MAY FIND LIQUIDS RANGING FROM MILK AND COOKING OIL TO PAINTS AND LIQUID SOAPS. IN INDUSTRY, USEFUL LIQUIDS INCLUDE CHEMICALS, DYES AND PETROLEUM FOR RUNNING ENGINES.

The atoms in a liquid are quite closely packed but not joined, so they can move past each other. This allows liquids to flow. All liquids share some basic properties:

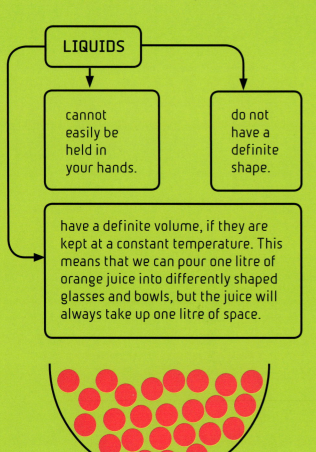

LIQUIDS

cannot easily be held in your hands.

do not have a definite shape.

have a definite volume, if they are kept at a constant temperature. This means that we can pour one litre of orange juice into differently shaped glasses and bowls, but the juice will always take up one litre of space.

TECHNOLOGY TALK

One property of liquids is that they expand when heated. We make use of this property in thermometers, which measure temperature. Liquid thermometers contain coloured alcohol. As the temperature rises, the alcohol expands, climbing up the markers of its tube. When the temperature falls, the alcohol contracts again.

Some liquids flow faster than others. Viscosity is the property of a liquid that describes how quickly or slowly it flows.

- Liquids with high viscosity look 'thick' and flow slowly. As the liquid flows, its atoms rub against each other, slowing it down. High-viscosity liquids include honey, motor oil and peanut butter. Peanut butter flows so slowly at room temperature that you might think it is a solid!

- Liquids with low viscosity look 'thin'. Their atoms rub together less as they flow. Low-viscosity liquids include water and milk.

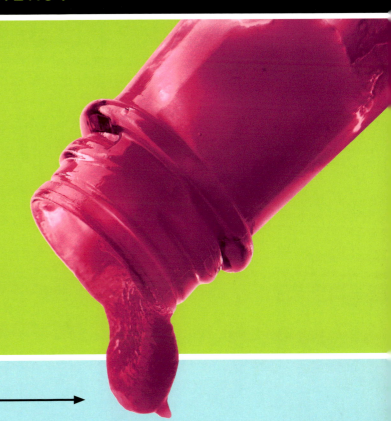

Ketchup is known for its frustratingly high viscosity!

PROJECT

A few liquids change their viscosity, depending on how much force you apply to them. They are called non-Newtonian fluids because they do not follow the rules of viscosity as worked out by the famous scientist Isaac Newton. Try making cornflour slime:

- In a large bowl or tray, mix 500 ml of water with 470 g of cornflour.

- Stir the slime slowly. It acts like a liquid because the particles of cornflour have time to move past each other.

- Punch the slime quickly. It feels hard, like a solid, and there is no splash of liquid. The water in the slime flows away from your punch, but the cornflour particles do not have time to move, leaving them packed in front of your fist.

GASES

NITROGEN IS THE MOST COMMON GAS ON EARTH, AS IT MAKES UP 78 PER CENT OF AIR. THE SECOND MOST COMMON IS OXYGEN, WHICH IS USED BY ANIMALS AND PLANTS TO PRODUCE ENERGY FOR LIFE.

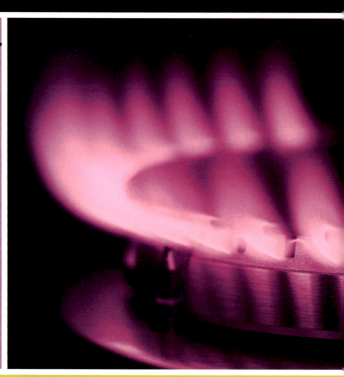

The atoms in a gas move around freely. They can be close to each other, or very far apart. As the atoms fly about, they bounce off each other and press against the walls of any container. This is called gas pressure. All gases share some basic properties:

GASES

- cannot be held in your hands.
- do not have a definite shape.
- do not have a definite volume. In any container, they will fill all the available space.

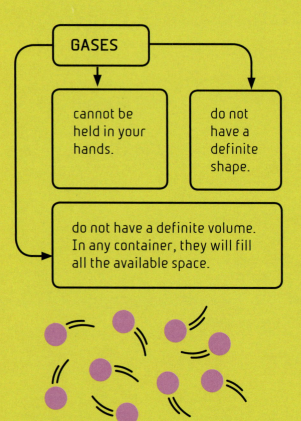

PROJECT

As the atoms in a gas get hotter, they move faster and hit the sides of their container more often. If a gas is in a flexible container, the pressure of the gas will make the container expand when the gas is warm, and contract when it is cool. Try this experiment:

■ Blow up a balloon and tie it. Measure the balloon's circumference with string.

■ Dunk the balloon in cold water for 10 minutes. Now measure the balloon's circumference. What has happened?

■ Hold the balloon over a heater for 10 minutes. Measure the balloon. What do you observe?

You probably use some gases regularly without even noticing. Two useful gases are:

- **CARBON DIOXIDE** The bubbles in a fizzy drink are carbon dioxide, which is a compound of the elements carbon and oxygen. The gas is mixed into the drink in a factory.

- **METHANE** A gas stove or oven is fuelled mainly by methane gas. Methane is a compound of carbon and hydrogen. It has the useful property of burning easily. Natural methane is found deep in the ground, then sent great distances along pipelines.

SCIENCE TALK

If you let go of a balloon filled with helium gas, it rises into the air. This is for the same reason that some solids float in liquids (see page 8). Helium is less dense than air – in other words, it is 'lighter' than air. In addition, the pressure of the air beneath the balloon is slightly greater than the pressure of the air above the balloon, because air gets thinner the higher you travel. That is why it is hard to breathe at the top of Mount Everest! The light balloon is pushed upward by the greater pressure of the air beneath it.

MELTING AND FREEZING

THE STATE OF A MATERIAL – SOLID, LIQUID OR GAS – DEPENDS ON ITS TEMPERATURE. MELTING AND FREEZING ARE CHANGES OF STATE.

All the pure elements, along with some other materials, can be melted. Materials that melt include water, metals, glass, rubber, wax and butter. Many other materials cannot be melted. For example, if you tried to melt wood by heating it, it would catch fire.

- As a solid gets warmer, its atoms are given more energy. They move faster and start to separate from each other. Eventually the solid melts, becoming a liquid.

- Freezing is the reverse process. When a liquid gets colder, its atoms have less energy. They slow down and move closer until they join together.

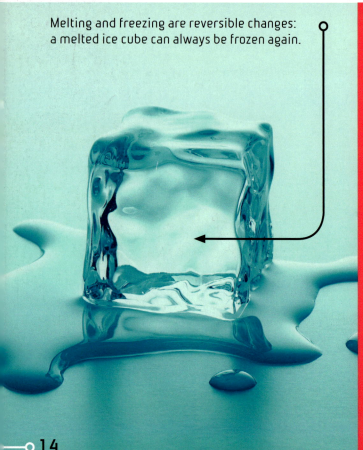

Melting and freezing are reversible changes: a melted ice cube can always be frozen again.

" MATHS TALK

The melting and freezing point of water is 0°C. This means that below 0°C, water is ice. However, water can be made to freeze at a lower temperature by mixing in another material, such as salt. If water is 10 per cent salt (nine spoonfuls of water for one spoonful of salt), the saltwater will freeze at -6°C. That is why road workers spread salt or grit on icy roads.

Every element has a different melting and freezing point:

- Gold freezes and melts at 1,064°C. If it were not a solid at room temperature, gold would be useless in jewellery!

- Mercury freezes and melts at -39°C. In the past, mercury was used in thermometers (see page 10), because it did not freeze until the temperature fell way below 0°C. Mercury is now known to be poisonous, so it is rarely used today.

SCIENCE TALK

The Earth is covered in a crust of cool, solid rock. However, deeper inside the Earth, in a region called the mantle, it is so hot that the rock becomes liquid. This runny rock is called magma. Sometimes magma is forced to the surface and thrown from a volcano. It is now called lava. When the lava cools, it hardens into solid rock.

EVAPORATING

EVAPORATION AND CONDENSATION ARE ALSO CHANGES OF STATE. EVAPORATION IS WHEN A LIQUID CHANGES INTO A GAS. CONDENSATION IS THE REVERSE: WHEN A GAS CHANGES INTO A LIQUID.

Evaporation happens because some atoms at the surface of a liquid are always moving fast enough to escape from it, changing into a gas. Little by little, any liquid will evaporate. We can speed up evaporation by heating a liquid: heat makes the atoms move faster so they escape more quickly. Evaporation happens really fast when we boil a liquid. When boiling, the atoms in the liquid move so quickly that they form bubbles of gas that rise to the surface and escape. The boiling point is the temperature at which a particular liquid boils.

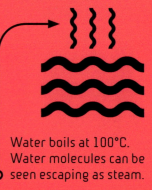

Water boils at 100°C. Water molecules can be seen escaping as steam.

ART TALK

Evaporation has a role to play in painting. When we put paint on paper, it is a liquid. Slowly, the water or other liquid in the paint evaporates. Grains of solid pigment (which give paint its colour) are left behind, stuck to the paper.

Condensation happens when a gas is cooled to its boiling point or below. As the gas cools, some of its atoms slow down and move closer together, becoming liquid. Evaporation and condensation are reversible changes, because an evaporated liquid can be condensed again.

When water vapour in the air touches the surface of a cool bottle, it condenses into droplets of water.

SCIENCE *TALK*

We can see evaporation and condensation at work in the Earth's water cycle. Water constantly evaporates from seas, rivers and lakes, forming the gas water vapour, which floats invisibly through the air. When the water vapour cools, it condenses into tiny droplets of water, which we can see as clouds. When the droplets grow too big and heavy to float in the air, they fall as rain.

WATER CONDENSES TO FORM CLOUDS

WATER CONSTANTLY EVAPORATES FROM THE SEA

MIXTURES

MAKING A MIXTURE IS QUITE SIMPLE: MIX TOGETHER TWO OR MORE DIFFERENT MATERIALS. A MIXTURE CAN ALWAYS BE SEPARATED BACK INTO ITS DIFFERENT MATERIALS.

Common mixtures include salad dressing, which is a mix of oil and vinegar; seawater, which is a mix of water, salt and other minerals; and air, which is a mix of different gases. Mixtures are different from compounds (see page 7):

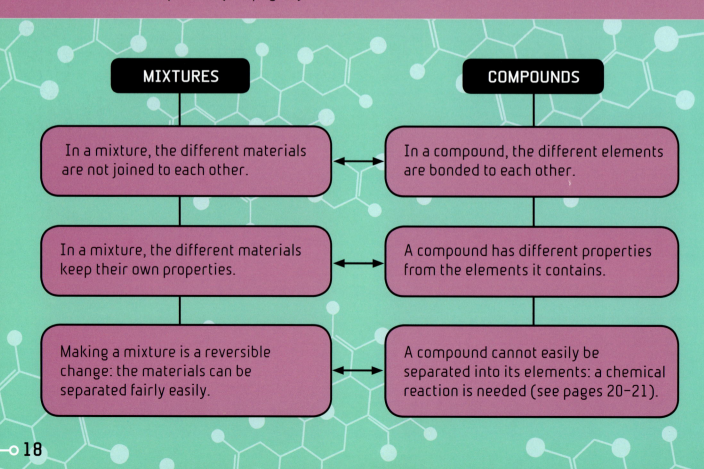

MIXTURES	COMPOUNDS
In a mixture, the different materials are not joined to each other.	In a compound, the different elements are bonded to each other.
In a mixture, the different materials keep their own properties.	A compound has different properties from the elements it contains.
Making a mixture is a reversible change: the materials can be separated fairly easily.	A compound cannot easily be separated into its elements: a chemical reaction is needed (see pages 20–21).

THINKING OUTSIDE THE BOX!

Different methods can be used to separate mixtures. A liquid mixture like oil and vinegar can be separated by letting the oil, which is less dense, rise to the surface, then draining the vinegar. Air is separated using a similar method, after cooling it to a liquid. Solids of different sizes can be separated with a sieve. A mixture of a liquid and an insoluble solid (see below) can be separated with a filter, which has tiny holes that let only the liquid pass through. Which methods would you use to separate: sand and gravel, oil and water, or sand and water?

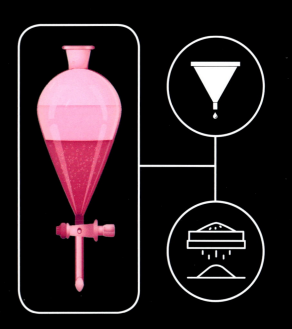

When some solids are mixed with water, they seem to disappear. That is because they spread evenly through the water, which is called dissolving. The water and the solid form a transparent liquid mixture called a solution. Some solids can dissolve in other liquids, but water is the best solvent: thousands of materials dissolve in it.

Solids that dissolve in water are said to be soluble in water. They include salt, sugar and coffee powder.

Solids that are insoluble in water include sand, flour and pepper. If mixed with water, they can still be seen, sitting at the bottom or floating on the top.

PROJECT

A solution can be separated into its different materials using evaporation. Make a saltwater solution to find out how:

- In a glass, mix a spoonful of salt with five or six spoonfuls of water.

- Leave the solution on a warm windowsill for a few days.

- What has happened to the water? What has happened to the salt?

Seawater is a solution containing salt, but sand is insoluble.

NO CHANGING BACK

SOME CHANGES ARE IRREVERSIBLE, BECAUSE THEY CANNOT BE UNDONE. DURING THE CHANGE, NEW MATERIALS ARE FORMED.

Irreversible changes are caused by chemical reactions. In a chemical reaction, two or more materials react to each other, forming changed bonds between their atoms. In the process, new compounds are made.

- Heating a material can cause an irreversible change. For example, when you heat bread, its molecules break apart, forming a new material: toast. Signs of the chemical reaction include a change in colour and in texture.

- Burning a material is an irreversible change. For example, ashes cannot be changed back into wood.

Burning wood is a useful chemical reaction, because it releases heat and light.

THINKING OUTSIDE THE BOX!

If you thought that matter was destroyed in a fire, think again. Atoms are never destroyed in a chemical reaction. They just separate or join together in different ways. When wood burns, it reacts with oxygen in the air. Wood contains the elements carbon, hydrogen and oxygen. The results of the chemical reaction are the release of the gas carbon dioxide (containing carbon and oxygen) and water vapour (containing hydrogen and oxygen). Ashes, which are the bits of wood that will not burn, are left behind. Energy is also released in the form of heat and light.

As we saw on pages 18–19, mixing materials does not always bring about a chemical reaction. However, some materials do react to each other just by touching:

- Iron reacts slowly with the oxygen and water in damp air, creating rust.
- A cut apple reacts quickly to the oxygen in air, which turns it brown.

Iron rusts more quickly at the seaside because the air contains lots of water vapour.

PROJECT

When vinegar and bicarbonate of soda are mixed together, a chemical reaction produces the gas carbon dioxide. Test this out by making a 'volcano':

- Place a plastic cup in a tray. Decorate the outside of the cup as a volcano, using cardboard, paints, leaves and twigs.
- Put 4 tablespoons of bicarbonate of soda into the cup.
- Pour 250 ml of vinegar into a measuring jug. You can add a few drops of red food colouring.
- Pour the vinegar into the cup. Step back and watch the 'eruption' of carbon dioxide!

CHEMICAL REACTIONS ARE TAKING PLACE ALL AROUND YOU. SOME REACTIONS ARE USEFUL, WHILE OTHERS ARE ALSO BEAUTIFUL.

LEAVES

Green plants make their food with a chemical reaction called photosynthesis. A plant's leaves are green because they contain a lot of the chemical chlorophyll, which absorbs energy from sunlight. The energy powers a chemical reaction between the carbon dioxide that the plant takes from the air, and water taken from the soil through the plant's roots. During the reaction, a sugar called glucose is made, which is food for the plant. Photosynthesis is the first link in a food chain that includes the animals that eat plants, and the animals that prey on plant-eaters.

FIREWORKS

When the fuse on a firework is lit, the heat sets off a chemical reaction between an explosive material, such as gunpowder, and oxygen in the air. The reaction releases gas, which rushes out behind the firework, forcing it into the air. The fuse continues to burn. When the heat reaches a second compartment of gunpowder, another explosion is set off, creating light and sound. Colours are made by burning compounds containing metals: for example, copper compounds create blue sparks.

DIGESTION

In your digestive system, chemical reactions break down large food molecules into smaller molecules that can be absorbed by the blood and passed round the body. Chemicals called enzymes react with particular food molecules. For example, the enzyme carbohydrase is found in saliva and in the small intestine. It breaks big starch molecules (found in potatoes and pasta) into simple sugars.

DECOMPOSITION

Decomposition is often called 'rotting'. It happens to old food and dead plants and animals. Decomposition is nature's way of recycling! It involves a series of chemical reactions caused by enzymes made in the bodies of 'decomposers' such as bacteria, insects and earthworms. Decomposers feed on dead material, leaving behind nutrients in their waste. Decomposition turns waste materials into nutrients for the soil. Nutrients are elements such as carbon, nitrogen and phosphorus that give plants some of the food they need to grow.

FORENSIC TESTS

Chemical reactions are used by forensics teams to investigate crime scenes. For example, the element iodine reacts to the oil and sweat in fingerprints, turning a print orange so it can be seen more clearly. The chemical luminol glows when it reacts to the iron in blood, which can reveal a bloodstain even when someone has tried to clean it up.

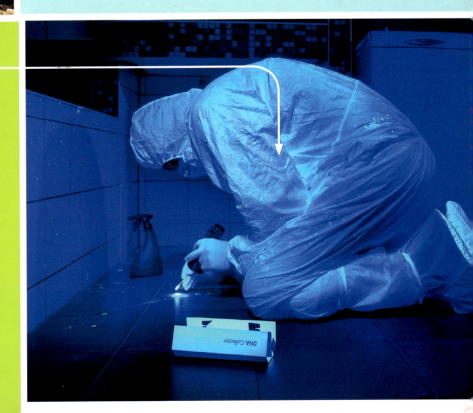

MINERALS AND ROCKS

MINERALS ARE SOLIDS THAT FORM NATURALLY IN THE GROUND OR IN WATER. ROCKS ARE MIXTURES OF DIFFERENT MINERALS.

Minerals are made of elements. Most minerals are formed when elements join together, but some – the metals – contain just one element. Some minerals, such as quartz, grow in molten magma (see page 15) as it cools into a solid. Other minerals, such as gypsum, grow as water evaporates, leaving behind any solid material.
Minerals grow in regular shapes called crystals.
They have many uses:

Salt, which has a strong taste, is sprinkled on food.

Diamond, which is the hardest natural material, is used in jewellery.

Mica is powdered and added to lipsticks because it is sparkly.

Graphite is used for the 'lead' in pencils because it is so soft it leaves a trail.

The mineral quartz is made from the elements silicon and oxygen.

TECHNOLOGY TALK

If you pass electricity through the mineral quartz, it vibrates exactly 32,768 times per second. Many watches contain a tiny quartz crystal. The watch's battery sends electricity to the crystal. The crystal's vibration is used to generate regular electric pulses, one per second. These pulses turn gears that spin the watch's hands, or power a display, giving the time in numbers.

The different properties of rocks make them suitable for different uses:

◄ **SLATE** is easily split into sheets and is impermeable, which means it does not allow liquid to pass through it. It is used to make roof tiles.

◄ **GRANITE** is strong and does not wear away easily. It is often used for building.

◄ **MARBLE** is smooth and can be beautifully patterned. It is often carved into sculptures.

◄ **COAL** burns easily, so it is used as a fuel. Unfortunately, coal releases carbon dioxide as it burns, which helps to trap heat in the atmosphere, causing global warming.

SCIENCE TALK

There are three groups of rocks: igneous, sedimentary and metamorphic. Each group formed in a different way. Igneous rock forms when hot, runny magma cools. Igneous rocks can form below the ground, or after magma bursts onto the Earth's surface as lava. Basalt is a common igneous rock. Sedimentary rocks are made when minerals, pebbles or dead animals and plants are pressed together until they harden. Limestone is a common sedimentary rock, made from seashells and coral. Metamorphic rocks are made when any type of rock is changed by great heat or pressure. For example, marble is limestone that has been heated.

Marble is a metamorphic rock that is easy to carve.

METAL

METALS ARE USED IN CONSTRUCTION, MACHINERY, WIRING, CUTLERY, PANS, JEWELLERY, COINS, ART AND MUCH MORE.

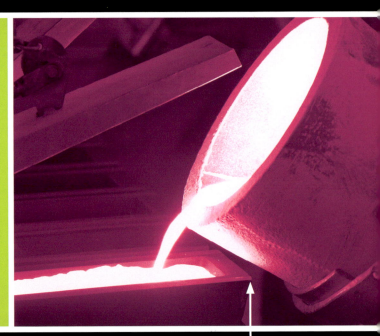

Molten gold can be poured into a mould.

Metals are elements and also minerals, as they are found in the ground as solids. There are 91 natural metals. The precious metals, which are rare and expensive, include silver, gold and platinum. The most common metals in the Earth's crust include aluminium and iron. Metals have many useful properties:

- They are shiny, strong and hard.
- They can be bent and hammered into different shapes without breaking. They can also be melted, poured into a shaped mould, then cooled into a solid.
- They are good conductors of heat and electricity (see page 9).
- Some metals, such as iron, are magnetic.

SCIENCE TALK

Only iron and similar metals, including nickel and cobalt, are magnetic. They are attracted to magnets and can be magnetised to become magnets. All atoms have tinier particles called electrons spinning round them, usually in random directions. When the electrons all spin in one direction, an invisible force called magnetism is created. Magnetic metals can become magnets on their own, or by being stroked many times by a magnet. Magnets have a north pole and south pole. The north pole of one magnet attracts the south pole, and repels the north pole, of another magnet.

ORES Metals are sometimes found in a pure form, but are more often mixed with rocks and other minerals. When these rocks and minerals contain large amounts of a useful metal, they are called ores. Ores are dug from the ground in a mine or quarry, then heated and processed to extract the metal.

ALLOYS An alloy is a manmade mixture of metals or of a metal with other elements. Alloys possess a mix of the useful properties of their ingredients. Cupronickel, an alloy of the metals copper, nickel and manganese, is used for coins. It is stronger than copper, harder-wearing than nickel, and easier to shape than manganese.

ENGINEERING TALK

Steel is an alloy of iron and the element carbon. Iron is a relatively weak metal, but is easy to work with. Carbon is extremely strong: one form of carbon is diamond. Steel therefore has great strength and is resistant to being stretched out of shape. These properties make it useful in construction, where it forms the frames that support skyscrapers. Steel is one of the world's most common materials, with 1.3 billion tonnes produced every year.

WOOD

THERE ARE ABOUT 1 TRILLION TONNES OF WOOD IN THE WORLD. HOWEVER, FOR EVERY TREE WE CUT DOWN, WE MUST PLANT .... AT LEAST ONE MORE TO PREVENT DEFORESTATION.

Wood is found in the trunks, branches and roots of trees and shrubs. It is made of fibres of cellulose crisscrossed with lignin. These are both strong polymers (see page 32), which are made of long, chain-like molecules. The useful properties of wood include:

- It is strong, flexible and long-lasting.
- It is easily cut and shaped.
- It is an insulator from heat and electricity (see page 9).
- It is easy to burn.

MATHS TALK

Wood was our first source of energy: humans started to burn wood to keep warm and cook food around 400,000 years ago. Other fuels, such as coal, gas and petroleum, have since been discovered, along with methods of harnessing renewable energy such as sunlight, wind and water. Renewable energies will not run out, unlike coal, gas and petroleum. Wood is a renewable energy as long as more trees are planted. Wood still provides 9 per cent of the world's energy, mostly in poorer regions. Try creating a pie chart showing the percentages of different energy sources you would like to see the world using by the year 2100.

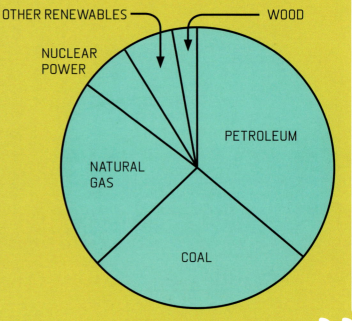

World energy sources today

OTHER RENEWABLES — WOOD
NUCLEAR POWER
PETROLEUM
NATURAL GAS
COAL

Paper is made from mashed wood, called pulp. The cellulose fibres are made wet, then pressed together into sheets.

Furniture is made from hard-wearing woods. Some, such as teak and rosewood, are also richly coloured.

Musical instruments, sports equipment, utensils and sculptures are carved from carefully chosen woods. For example, white willow is used for cricket bats because it is light but strong.

Construction materials are made from strong wood known as timber. When timber is strengthened with layers of glue, it is called engineered wood.

Paper is pressed and rolled at a paper mill.

TECHNOLOGY TALK

It is important to recycle paper and other wood products to slow down deforestation. Used paper is mixed with water and chemicals to break it down into a slush of cellulose fibres. It is cleaned, pressed and dried. However, paper can be recycled only seven times before the cellulose fibres become too broken. Recycled paper is used for lower-quality wood products, such as newspapers, packaging and insulation.

GLASS

GLASS IS USED FOR OBJECTS THAT NEED TO BE TRANSPARENT, SUCH AS WINDOWS AND WINDSCREENS, LIGHT BULBS, COMPUTER SCREENS, DRINKING VESSELS AND PACKAGING SUCH AS BOTTLES AND JARS.

Glass is a manmade material with three major ingredients: sand, limestone and soda ash. These inorganic materials are melted in a furnace at a temperature of 1,700°C. Glass has many useful properties:

- It is transparent and colourless.
- It is strong and long-lasting, although it is brittle, which means it can shatter. This is why glass has been replaced by plastic in most spectacle lenses.
- When molten, glass can be formed into any shape.
- It is waterproof and does not react to most chemicals.

" ART TALK

The glass-blowers of Venice, Italy, are famous for their intricate glass products, from tiny animals to vases. They use the traditional technique of inflating glass into a bubble, using a blowpipe. This is possible because liquid glass has high viscosity: the atoms do not separate when blown. Metal tools are used to tweak and pull the liquid glass into shapes. As it cools, the glass hardens into a solid. "

The properties of glass can be altered with extra ingredients or techniques:

- Ordinary glass is transparent because light passes through it, bending only a little as it does. Crystal glass has ingredients that increase the amount it bends light, creating a sparkle. Textures, coatings and backings make glass more opaque, to offer privacy or to create mirrors.

- Some modern glass contains ingredients or coatings to make it shatterproof or more resistant to heat, so it does not melt in the oven. Bulletproof glass is layered with flexible plastic, which helps it bend rather than shatter if struck.

- Glass can be coloured by adding extra ingredients. For example, iron oxide creates a green tint.

- Glass fibre is a textile made from threads of glass, which trap air between them. Heat travels slowly through air, so glass fibre is often used for insulation, to prevent heat escaping from homes.

This sparkly mouse is made from crystal glass.

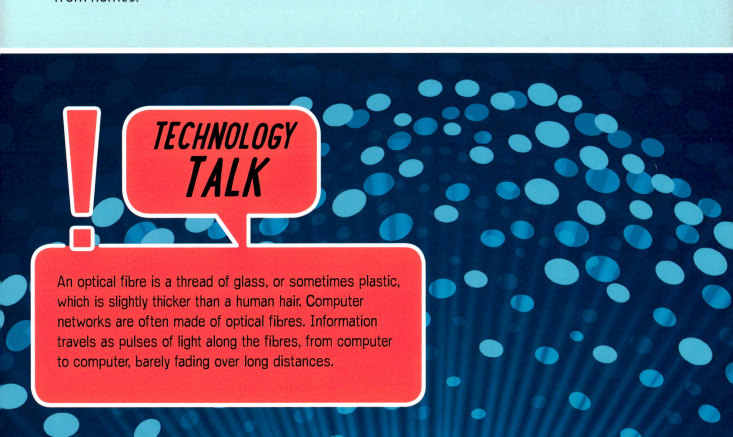

TECHNOLOGY TALK

An optical fibre is a thread of glass, or sometimes plastic, which is slightly thicker than a human hair. Computer networks are often made of optical fibres. Information travels as pulses of light along the fibres, from computer to computer, barely fading over long distances.

PLASTICS

PLASTICS ARE MANMADE MATERIALS. MOST PLASTICS ARE MADE FROM .... PETROLEUM, COAL AND NATURAL GAS – 'FOSSIL FUELS' THAT WERE FORMED OVER MILLIONS OF YEARS FROM THE REMAINS OF LIVING THINGS.

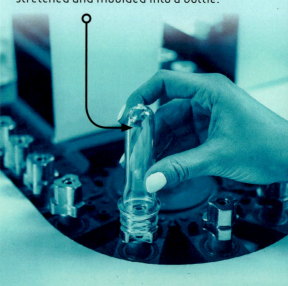

This hollow plastic 'preform' will be stretched and moulded into a bottle.

Plastics are made by the process of polymerisation, which links atoms into a chain, called a polymer. Polymerisation is done by creating chemical reactions between atoms, often at high temperature and under pressure. Plastics share properties with natural polymers, such as rubber (see page 34) and cellulose (see page 28), but only manmade polymers are called plastics. The properties of plastics include:

- They are strong and waterproof.
- They can be melted into any shape, then become rigid when cooled. Thermoplastics, such as polyethylene, can be melted and reshaped many times. Thermosetting plastics, such as melamine, can be shaped only once, as the polymer chains link into a rigid grid when heated.
- They can be dyed or made transparent.
- They are good insulators of heat and electricity (see page 9).

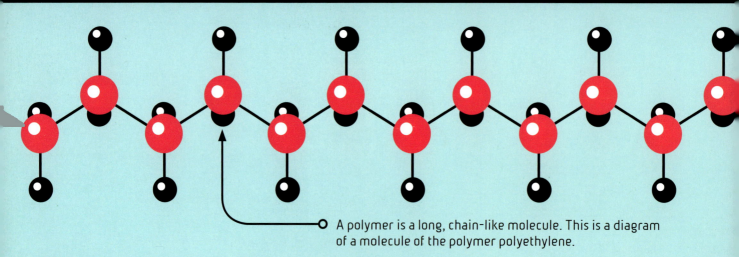

A polymer is a long, chain-like molecule. This is a diagram of a molecule of the polymer polyethylene.

THINKING OUTSIDE THE BOX!

Since most plastics are made from fossil fuels, which are not a renewable resource, today's materials engineers are looking at how to develop plastics from renewable raw materials, such as vegetable oils and cellulose. These are called bioplastics. One benefit of bioplastics is that they biodegrade, or decompose (see page 23), fairly quickly, unlike ordinary plastics.

This spoon and fork are made of bioplastic.

These are some of the most commonly used plastics:

POLYETHYLENE, made from the natural gas ethylene, is the most common plastic. It is made into bottles, containers and carrier bags.

PVC, or polyvinyl chloride, is made from the gas vinyl chloride. It is strong and hard, so is used for window frames, signs and pipes.

POLYSTYRENE is made from the oil styrene, which itself is made from petroleum. Polystyrene foams are soft and good insulators, so are used in packaging, food containers and insulation.

MELAMINE resin is a strong thermosetting plastic that is made into bowls and kitchenware, flooring and worktops.

MATHS TALK

Plastics are cheap to produce and extremely versatile, leading the world to make around 300 million tonnes each year. That is the same weight as 4 million adults. Around 50 per cent of this plastic is just used once, then thrown away. It is estimated that 8 million tonnes of plastic is dumped into our oceans every year, where it can entangle or be eaten by sea creatures.

★ ★ ★

HALL OF FAME: POLYMERS

PLASTICS ARE NOT THE ONLY USEFUL POLYMERS: OTHER MANMADE AND NATURAL POLYMERS HAVE AMAZING PROPERTIES. THESE LONG MOLECULES TANGLE WITH EACH OTHER, CREATING PROPERTIES, SUCH AS ELASTICITY AND THE ABILITY TO FORM FIBRES, THAT WOULD BE IMPOSSIBLE WITH SHORT MOLECULES.

RUBBER

Natural rubber is harvested from rubber trees in the form of latex – a sticky liquid that is collected by cutting the bark. The latex is processed and coagulates, or dries and sticks together, into rubber. Rubber is elastic, which means it can be stretched and then springs back into shape. It is also waterproof and flexible. It is used for rubber bands, tyres, hoses, insulation and rainwear.

GLUE

Many glues make use of the natural stickiness of some polymers. Polymers can be sticky because their long chains are good at getting into the tiny cracks and holes in other substances, and they also have the strength to resist breaking when pulled. Craft glue is made of the polymer polyvinyl acetate (PVA) dissolved in a liquid. When the glue is spread onto a material, it is absorbed by it. As the liquid evaporates, the polymer chains link together, hardening and sticking to the material.

NYLON

Nylons are a group of polymers invented by US chemist Wallace Carothers in 1935. Although nylons can be produced in many forms, they are most well known as a fibre, which is made into tights and other clothing, carpets, umbrellas and seatbelts. Nylon is very strong, long-lasting and waterproof.

WOOL

Wool is the hair that forms a sheep's coat. The coat can be shorn, then spun into a fibre for making clothing, blankets, carpets and insulation. Wool contains the polymer keratin, which is also found in nails and hooves. Its long chains make it possible to twist wool into a strong thread that holds together. The chains also make wool slightly elastic. In addition, wool traps air between its fibres, making it a good insulator.

FIMO®

Fimo® is a modelling clay that contains the polymer PVC, mixed with liquid ingredients that make it easy to shape at room temperature. When it is pressed, the clay flows like a liquid, but when the force is removed, the clay holds its new shape, like a solid. It is then baked in an oven to make it rigid.

TEXTILES

TEXTILES ARE MATERIALS MADE FROM INTERLACED NATURAL OR MANMADE FIBRES, OR THREADS. THE FIBRES ARE LACED TOGETHER USING TECHNIQUES SUCH AS WEAVING AND KNITTING.

Natural fibres come from plants or animals:

PLANT FIBRES The most commonly used plant fibre is cotton, made from the fluffy coating around the seeds of cotton plants. Its softness makes the fibre ideal for clothing. Bast fibres, which are tougher than cotton, come from the stems of plants, including flax (made into linen) and hemp. These make coarser clothes, rugs and packaging. The hardest plant fibres are taken from a plant's leaves, such as raffia from palms and sisal from agave. They are used for bags, hats and rugs.

ANIMAL FIBRES Wool is the most commonly used animal fibre, but other soft and warm animal-hair fibres include mohair and cashmere from goats, and angora from rabbits. Silk comes from the cocoon spun by silkworms as a protective casing while they change from caterpillars to moths. Silk is extremely smooth and strong.

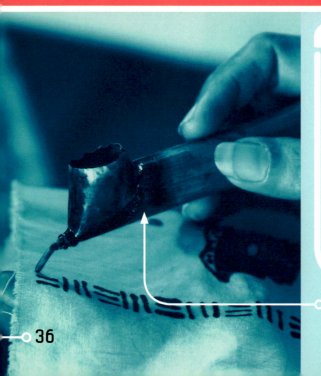

" ART TALK

Patterns can be created by weaving together fibres that have been dyed different colours. Tartan cloth is made in this way. Some textiles are dyed after they have been woven. For example, tie-dyeing is when areas of cloth are tied or twisted before dipping in dye, creating a spiralling or marbled effect. A traditional Indonesian textile-dyeing method is called batik. Parts of the design are coated in dye-resistant wax before the cloth is dipped in dye. "

Wax is applied to cloth using the batik technique.

The most commonly used manmade fabrics are polyester, nylon (see page 35), acrylic and olefin. They are all factory-made polymers, with fossil fuels as their raw materials. To make them, liquid chemicals are forced through tiny holes. As the liquid exits the holes, it dries into threads. Polyester is often mixed with natural fibres, such as cotton, to make a wrinkle-resistant fabric. Acrylic is warm and soft, making a cheaper alternative to wool. Olefin is quick-drying, stain-resistant, warm and lightweight. It is often sold under different names, depending on its use, in products from sportswear to teabags, ropes to carpet.

This olefin tennis shirt dries quickly when it gets sweaty.

PROJECT

Examine the labels on your school uniform or a friend's to find out which fibres they contain. With an adult's permission, use the Internet to do some research:

- Are the fibres natural, manmade or a mix?

- Which plants, animals or raw materials were the fibres obtained from?

- Have the textiles been given any coatings or treatments to give them special properties, such as being resistant to stains, wrinkles or water?

CERAMICS

CERAMICS ARE MADE BY BAKING INORGANIC MATERIALS IN A VERY HOT KILN OR OVEN. THE MOST WELL-KNOWN CERAMICS ARE PRODUCED BY HEATING CLAY, BUT THERE ARE PLENTY OF OTHERS.

Clay is a soft rock, formed from minerals and decayed plants mixed with water. It is easy to mould when wet. When heated, the water evaporates and the clay atoms bond together into a rigid solid. Clay ceramics include bricks, pottery and tiles. Pottery and tiles are often coated with a tough glaze, which can be coloured, to make them more waterproof and harder to scratch. All ceramics share some properties:

- They are strong, hard and long-lasting, but they are brittle.
- They are good insulators of heat and electricity.
- They can withstand sudden changes in temperature without melting or cracking.
- Unlike glass, ceramics cannot be melted and reshaped.

"ART TALK

Pottery is so hard-wearing that some clay objects have survived for thousands of years. We can learn about ancient peoples from the shapes of their pottery and the designs painted on it. Ancient potters made statues of goddesses and gods, which tell us a little about what they believed; pots and jars to hold food, decorated with plants, animals, dancers, sportspeople and stories; and beads, toys and games. "

Not all modern ceramics use clay as their main ingredient. Some are made from carefully chosen elements that give them extraordinary strength and hardness. Products made from ceramics include:

BULLETPROOF VESTS are made from boron carbide, a manmade compound of the elements carbon and boron. It is one of the hardest known materials. The ingredients must be heated in a furnace to over 2,763°C.

KITCHEN KNIVES can be made of the ceramic zirconia, a compound of the elements zirconium (a metal) and oxygen. It is exceptionally strong, so it stays sharper than steel knives.

PROJECT

Work out a series of tests to compare the properties of a range of solids:

- Gather a collection of materials that includes some or all of the following: rocks, minerals, metals, wood, glass, plastics, textiles and ceramics.

- Design five tests that allow you to determine if the materials have these properties: hardness, solubility, transparency, heat conduction and magnetism. You may need safety glasses and an adult's help to carry out some tests.

- Draw up a table, or a Venn diagram, to show your results.

COMPOSITES

COMPOSITES ARE MADE FROM TWO OR MORE MATERIALS, WHICH REMAIN SEPARATE IN THE RESULTING MIXTURE. MOST COMPOSITES CONTAIN A STRONG MATERIAL, SUCH AS WOOD, BOUND TOGETHER WITH ANOTHER MATERIAL, SUCH AS GLUE.

In a composite, the strong material is often called the 'reinforcement', while the material that surrounds it is called the 'binder'. The reinforcement is usually positioned in a grid or in layers to make the composite stronger. Early composites were often used in construction, and they are still widely used in building today:

WATTLE AND DAUB

This composite material has been used for building walls for at least 6,000 years. Wooden strips are woven together, then 'daubed' with a sticky material such as straw mixed with dung or clay.

CONCRETE

The ancient Romans used concrete to build structures such as the Colosseum, some of which still stand today. Concrete is made by mixing crushed rock with sand, water and cement. Cement is made by heating powdered limestone and clay. Chemical reactions are set off in the mixture, which sets hard.

ENGINEERING TALK

Reinforced concrete is a composite material made by pouring concrete around a grid of steel cables. The resulting mix has the strength of concrete, plus the strength of steel. Steel is strong when stretched, but not as strong when squashed. Concrete is strong when squashed, but weak when stretched. Reinforced concrete is strong whether squashed or stretched!

The extraordinary shape of the Sagrada Família church, in Barcelona, Spain, was made possible by reinforced concrete.

Materials engineers have continued to develop new composite materials with very useful properties:

FIBREGLASS

Fibreglass has glass fibres as its reinforcement and plastic as its binder. The glass fibres may be woven or layered. Fibreglass is strong, lightweight and can be moulded. It is used in aircraft, cars, surfboards and roofing.

CARBON FIBRE

Carbon fibre is plastic reinforced with fibres of carbon. This composite is more expensive than fibreglass but even lighter and stronger. It is used in spacecraft, construction and running blades for disabled athletes.

! TECHNOLOGY TALK

A cermet is a composite containing a ceramic ('cer') with a metal ('met') binder. It has the useful properties of ceramics, such as hardness and withstanding high temperatures. It combines these with the useful properties of metals, such as being mouldable. One use for cermets is the exterior of spacecraft, which must cope with extreme changes in temperature.

The noses of spacecraft are often made from high-performance cermets.

★ ★ ★

THESE INVENTORS CREATED NEW MATERIALS WITH INCREDIBLY USEFUL PROPERTIES. SOME OF THEIR INVENTIONS ARE IN EVERY HOME – WHILE OTHERS ARE JUST STARTING TO CHANGE THE WORLD.

CHARLES MACINTOSH (1766–1843)

In 1824, Scottish inventor Charles Macintosh invented a method of waterproofing fabric. The waterproof raincoat, or 'mac', is named after him. His invention was to stick together two pieces of fabric with rubber (see page 34). Rubber is impermeable. Not all modern raincoats use Macintosh's method: some use manmade textiles that are waterproof.

STEPHANIE KWOLEK (1923–2014)

Stephanie Kwolek was a US chemist who invented a fibre called Kevlar in 1965. Like other manmade fibres, it is a polymer created in a laboratory. What makes Kevlar special is that it is five times stronger than steel, but light enough to be worn. It is used to make body armour, bicycle tyres and sails for racing yachts.

HARRY BREARLEY (1871-1948)

The drawback of ordinary steel is that it rusts, because it contains iron (see page 21). Inventor Harry Brearley grew up and worked in Sheffield, England, where cutlery had been made since the 16th century. In 1913, Brearley invented stainless steel, initially called 'rustless steel', which does not easily rust or stain when exposed to oxygen and water. Stainless steel contains chromium, which forms a film on the surface to protect the steel. It is widely used for cutlery.

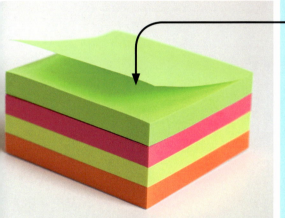

SPENCER SILVER (1931-)

A US chemist, Spencer Silver invented the glue that is used in Post-It notes, first sold in 1980. The glue is strong enough to hold papers together, weak enough to let the papers be torn apart, and can be used again and again. The glue is pressure-sensitive, which means it needs only to be pressed down to stick, and unsticks when pulled away. It is made of minute sticky spheres, which are unbreakable.

ANDRE GEIM (1958-) AND CONSTANTIN NOVOSELOV (1974-)

These scientists at the University of Manchester, England, found a way to produce the material graphene in 2004. Graphene is two-dimensional (flat) and consists only of a hexagonal grid of carbon atoms. The grid can go on and on for ever. Graphene is nearly transparent but is 200 times stronger than steel. In the future, it could make giant sieves to separate salt from seawater. In coastal regions, these could provide drinking water for millions of people.

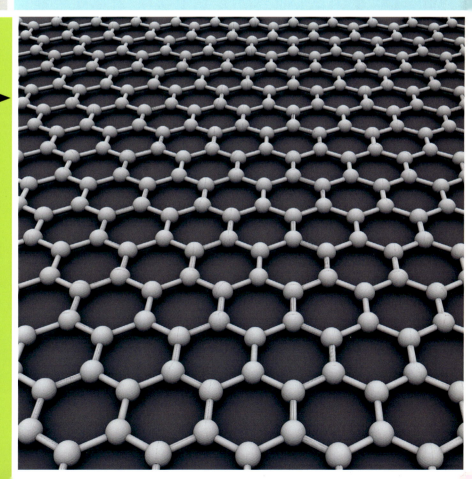

RECYCLING

RECYCLING INVOLVES SORTING PRODUCTS INTO THEIR RAW MATERIALS, PROCESSING THOSE MATERIALS TO MAKE THEM SUITABLE FOR REUSE, THEN TURNING THEM INTO NEW PRODUCTS.

There are several reasons why recycling materials is essential:

- Many materials are unsustainable, which means they will run out. Unsustainable materials include metals, minerals and fossil fuels. Other materials, such as wood and cotton, are sustainable as long as we manage the rates at which we harvest and grow them.

- When we throw away materials rather than recycling them, they often end up in landfills. Landfill space will one day run out, and decaying waste in landfills releases the gas methane, which adds to global warming.

- Although recycling materials does consume energy, it usually consumes less energy and creates less pollution than collecting raw materials.

MATHS TALK

Nearly all waste can be recycled, although it is currently expensive or difficult to recycle some materials, such as ceramics and particular plastics. Composting, when organic waste is left to decompose, is also a form of recycling. Austria is the country with the highest recycling rate, at 63 per cent. The United Kingdom only recycles 39 per cent of its waste. Turkey and Chile are bottom of the list with recycling rates of 1 per cent.

RECYCLING MATERIALS

METAL
The most commonly recycled materials – metals – can be melted and reshaped without losing quality. Around 400 million tonnes of metal are recycled every year, with steel the most widely recycled of all.

PAPER
Measured by weight, a third of waste is paper, but only 10 per cent of new paper products are made from recycled paper. Paper can only be 'downcycled', or turned into products of less value (see 'Technology Talk' on page 29).

PLASTIC
Thermoplastics, such as polyethylene terephthalate (PET), used for plastic bottles, can be melted and reshaped into products of equal value. Thermosetting plastics can be ground up and used in composites and construction materials. The relatively new process of depolymerisation turns waste plastics into oil.

GLASS
Waste glass is crushed and melted to create new bottles and containers. Recycled glass is also used in insulation, artificial grass and ceramics.

TEXTILES
Clothing can be given to charities to be reworn. Textiles can also be shredded and recycled into fibre for mattress fillings and insulation. This is called fibre reclamation.

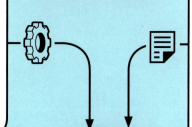

PROJECT

Design a product made entirely with recycled materials. Will you upcycle your materials by turning them into something of greater value, such as jewellery, clothing or furniture? Or will you downcycle them into something less expensive but perhaps lifesaving, like a mosquito net?

EcoARK, built in China in 2010, was a temporary exhibition hall made of recycled plastic bricks.

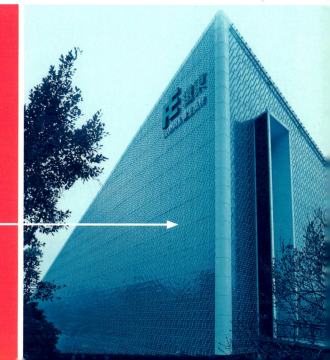

GLOSSARY

atoms the smallest parts of an element that can exist by themselves

brittle hard, but easily broken or cracked

chemical reaction a change that takes place when atoms of different elements rearrange themselves to form a new material

compound a material formed when the atoms of two or more elements bond to each other

condensation when a gas cools and becomes a liquid

conduction the process by which heat or electricity moves through a material, passing from atom to atom

decomposition the process of decaying, or separating into simpler materials or elements

dense having molecules that are closely packed

electrons tiny particles that spin around the nucleus of an atom

elements materials made entirely of just one type of atom

evaporation when a liquid turns into a gas

fibres threads

fossil fuels fuels such as coal, gas and petroleum, formed in the ground from the remains of living things

gas a state of matter in which atoms move freely and will expand to fill any container

impermeable not allowing liquid to pass through

inorganic not made of living things

insulators materials that do not allow heat or electricity to pass through easily

irreversible change a change caused by a chemical reaction, in which new materials are formed. The change cannot be turned back

liquid a state of matter in which atoms are quite closely packed but not joined, so liquids can flow

magma molten, liquid rock found below the Earth's surface

matter anything that takes up space and has mass (often called 'weight'). All matter is made of atoms

molecule a group of atoms that are bonded together

nucleus the centre of an atom

organic made from living things

polymers materials made of long, chain-like molecules

pressure a pressing force

renewable a natural material or source of energy that will not run out

reversible changes changes from one state to another, which can be turned back again

room temperature a comfortable indoor temperature

solid a state of matter in which atoms are joined together in a definite shape

soluble when a solid can mix with a liquid so that it seems to disappear

thermoplastics manmade polymers that can be melted and reshaped many times

thermosetting plastics manmade polymers that can be melted and shaped only once

viscosity a measure of how easily a liquid flows

volume the amount of space that a material takes up

water vapour water in the form of a gas

 FURTHER READING

Material Matters (Science is Everywhere) Rob Colson (Wayland, 2017)

Materials and Properties (Straight Forward with Science) Peter Riley (Franklin Watts, 2015)

Why Do Ice Cubes Float? (Science FAQ) Thomas Canavan (Franklin Watts, 2016)

 WEBSITES

FIND OUT MORE ABOUT MATERIALS AT THE FOLLOWING WEBSITES:

www.bbc.co.uk/bitesize/ks2/science/materials/

www.dkfindout.com/uk/science/materials/

www.recycling-guide.org.uk/

 QUIZ

- Which element is the lightest?

- Name a reversible change.

- Who invented nylon?

- What was the first manmade ceramic material?

- Which composite material did the Romans use to construct the Colosseum?

INDEX

QUIZ ANSWERS

- Hydrogen
- Reversible changes include melting, freezing, evaporating, condensing and mixing.
- Wallace Carothers
- Pottery
- Concrete

BUILDINGS

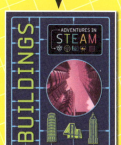

- Starting out ■ Materials
- Structure ■ Arches and domes
- Designing a building ■ Scale and plans ■ Perspective ■ Ancient buildings ■ Greeks and Romans
- Castles and cathedrals ■ Architects
- Houses ■ Eco-friendly buildings
- Skyscrapers ■ Landmarks
- Public buildings ■ Bridges
- Famous bridges ■ Tunnels
- When things go wrong
- Hostile conditions

COMPUTERS

- A Computer is... ■ Computers everywhere ■ Ones and zeros
- A computer's brain ■ Memory
- Inputs ■ Outputs ■ Programming
- Early days ■ Computer scientists
- Software ■ Graphics ■ Games
- Personal computers ■ Networks
- The web ■ Virtual reality
- Artificial intelligence ■ Amazing computers ■ A changed planet
- Future computers

MATERIALS

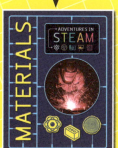

- Choosing Materials ■ Natural or Manmade ■ Solid ■ Liquid ■ Gas
- Rocks and Minerals ■ Wood
- Metal ■ Glass ■ Building
- Plastics ■ Ceramics ■ Textiles
- Art ■ Composites ■ Chemicals
- Super Materials ■ Special Surfaces
- Shape Changers ■ Recycling
- Future Materials

ROBOTS

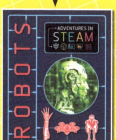

- Designing a robot ■ Moving parts
- Circuits ■ Sensors ■ Sight and navigation ■ Code ■ Programming robots ■ Artificial intelligence
- Robot ethics ■ The first robots
- Robots in danger ■ Robots in space
- Drones and cars ■ Real robots
- Household robots ■ Robots and medicine ■ Bionics ■ Robotic arms
- Androids ■ Fictional robots

SPACE

- Learning about space ■ Our solar system ■ Stars ■ Galaxies and the universe ■ Comets and meteors
- Black holes ■ The Big Bang
- Astronomers ■ Observatories and telescopes ■ Space exploration
- The science of space ■ Astronauts
- Training for space
- The International Space Station
- Space walks ■ Rockets ■ Rovers
- Space probes ■ Satellites
- Space colonies ■ Future exploration

VEHICLES

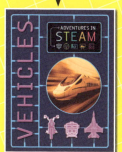

- Designing a vehicle ■ Land vehicles ■ Bicycles ■ Cars
- Famous cars ■ Trains ■ Watercraft
- Boats and ships ■ Hovercraft
- Aircraft ■ Aeroplanes
- Helicopters ■ Extreme terrain vehicles ■ Power ■ Materials
- Speed ■ Braking ■ Safety features
- Style ■ Record breakers
- Vehicles of the future